Brandon's
SO Bossy

First published in 2013 by Wayland
Text © Wayland 2013
Illustrations © Jack Hughes 2013

Wayland
338 Euston Road
London NW1 3BH

Wayland Australia
Level 17/207 Kent Street
Sydney, NSW 2000

Commissioning Editor: Victoria Brooker
Design: Lisa Peacock and Alyssa Peacock

British Library Cataloguing in Publication Data
Heneghan, Judith.
Brandon's SO bossy. -- (Dragon School)
1. Etiquette--Pictorial works--Juvenile fiction.
2. Children's stories--Pictorial works.
I. Title II. Series III. Hughes, Jack.
823.9'2-dc23

ISBN 978 0 7502 7959 8

Printed in China

Wayland is a division of Hachette Children's Books,
an Hachette UK Company
www.hachette.co.uk

Brandon's SO Bossy

Written by Judith Heneghan
Illustrated by Jack Hughes

WAYLAND

Brandon wasn't the biggest dragon
at Dragon School, but he was the bossiest.
He loved telling his friends what to do.

One day, Brandon discovered something exciting.

Dragon
Skills
Contest

'The Dragon Skills Contest is tomorrow!'
he told his friends. 'There are prizes for
flying, roaring and fire breathing!'

Dragon Skills Contest

'Yippee!' said Jasmine. 'I love flying! Let's practise!'
'Ooh yes!' agreed Noah and Ruby.

The three young dragons flew up towards
the clouds. They twirled and they swooped.
Jasmine even looped the loop.

'Come and join us, Brandon!'
she called as she hovered overhead.
But Brandon was frowning.

'Stop!' he shouted, bossily, zooming up
in front of them. 'Your flying is all wrong!
You're not doing it properly!
Follow me!'

So the other three dragons stopped twirling and swooping and loop the looping, and followed Brandon.

Brandon flew in straight lines, back and forth, back and forth, back and forth.

'This isn't much fun,' said Jasmine.

'I'd rather practise roaring,' said Noah.

'So would I!' agreed Ruby.

Noah flew down to the ground and took a deep breath. 'ROOAARR!' he roared, as loudly as he could. Jasmine and Ruby did the same.

RROOARRR!

Their roars echoed around the mountains.
'Wow, that sounds good,' said Noah.
'Come and join us, Brandon!'
But Brandon was annoyed.

'Stop!' he shouted. 'You're doing it all wrong!'
The other three dragons stopped roaring.

'You're being a bit bossy,' said Ruby.

'Well, that's because I know best!' said Brandon. He stuck out his chest and spread out his wings. 'Listen to me!'

His friends listened for a bit, but Brandon wouldn't let them join in. Soon they left him to practise by himself.

When Brandon had finished roaring,
he sat down on a rock. The forest was quiet.
He was alone. He wondered what the others
were doing.

Then he noticed smoke in the sky above the trees. The smoke made different shapes - a butterfly, a boat and a banana.

STOP!

Brandon followed the smoke shapes.
When he reached a clearing, he saw
his three friends. They were practising
their fire breathing without him!

'Stop!' he shouted, hurrying towards them.
'You're doing it all wrong! You're blowing
out too much fire! Watch me!'

The other dragons looked at each other.

'We wanted to practise by ourselves,' said Noah.

'You're always telling us what to do!' complained Jasmine.

'You're SO bossy!' added Ruby.

'Oh,' said Brandon. Ruby was right.
He'd wanted them to do everything his way.
'I'm sorry I was bossy,' he said. 'Jasmine is really
good at flying. Noah is great at roaring and Ruby is fantastic
at fire-breathing. You don't need me to tell you what to do.'

Ruby looked thoughtful for a minute. Then she grinned at Brandon. 'OF COURSE we need you!' she cried. 'I've just had a brilliant idea!'

The next day dawned bright and sunny.
Everyone gathered for the Dragon Skills
Contest. The prizes for flying, roaring
and fire breathing stood gleaming
on a table.

Brandon felt nervous,
and excited.
'Are you ready?'
whispered Ruby.

Brandon nodded and held up a flag.
'Ready, steady, GO!' he yelled
in his biggest, bossiest voice.

GO!

WHOOOOSH!

And this time, his friends did exactly what he told them!

Meet all the Dragons– Brandon, Jasmine, Noah and Ruby!

BRANDON'S SO BOSSY!
Judith Heneghan
Jack Hughes

978 0 7502 7959 8

JASMINE'S SO FUSSY!
Judith Heneghan
Jack Hughes

978 0 7502 7961 1

NOAH'S SO NOISY!
Judith Heneghan
Jack Hughes

978 0 7502 7960 4

RUBY'S SO RUDE!
Judith Heneghan
Jack Hughes

978 0 7502 7958 1